HEIR TO THE THRONE

Adapted by Kate Egan
Based on the Teleplay by Annie DeYoung
Based on the Story by David Morgasen and Annie DeYoung

Copyright © 2009 Disney Enterprises, Inc. All rights reserved. Published by Disney Press, an imprint of Disney Book Group.
No part of this book may be reproduced or transmitted in any form or by any means, electronic or mechanical, including
photocopying, recording, or by any information storage and retrieval system, without written permission from the publisher.
For information address Disney Press, 114 Fifth Avenue, New York, New York 10011-5690.

Printed in the United States of America
First Edition 1 2 3 4 5 6 7 8 9 10
Library of Congress Control Number on file
ISBN 978-1-4231-2283-8

For more Disney Press fun, visit www.disneybooks.com
Visit DisneyChannel.com

If you purchased this book without a cover, you should be aware that this book is stolen property. It was reported as "unsold and destroyed"
to the publisher, and neither the author nor the publisher has received any payment for this "stripped" book.

Disney PRESS
New York

In the small nation of Costa Luna, it was a special day. Sixteen-year-old Princess Rosalinda Marie Montoya Fiore was dressed up in her finest gown. Later that month, she would be crowned queen. Now she was practicing for the ceremony so everything would be perfect on the big day.

The rehearsal was going well until General Kane arrived. He was the ruler of a nearby country, and he wanted to rule Costa Luna, too.

Rosalinda's mother, Sophia, had hired a secret agent named Major Mason to protect Rosalinda.

When General Kane tried to capture the princess, Major Mason rescued her and helped her escape. He brought her to the headquarters of the Princess Protection Program.

The P.P.P. was a top secret organization that rescued princesses and gave them new identities until it was safe for them to return home.

Rosalinda would go undercover as an average American girl named Rosie Gonzalez. Unlike most P.P.P. princesses, she would stay with Major Mason and his daughter, Carter, in Louisiana.

In Louisiana, Carter was surprised to see Rosie in her bedroom.

"What are you doing here?" asked Carter.

"Major Mason gave me this room," Rosie explained.

Carter was not happy, especially when her father told her she had to help Rosie blend in.

At bedtime, Rosie asked for a nightgown. "Preferably silk. Preferably pink," she said.

Carter gave her some pajamas. They were not like anything Rosie would normally wear.

At breakfast, no one served the meal. Rosie didn't even know where to begin to find something to eat.

Rosie didn't fit in at school, either. None of her classmates cared that she could speak six languages. She ate a hamburger with a knife and fork. Plus, she had never heard of a homecoming dance!

The whole school was going to vote for three princesses. At the dance, one of them would be crowned homecoming queen.

"You vote for royalty here?" Rosie asked Carter. "So anyone can be a princess? Even you?"

Carter rolled her eyes.

Carter tried to help her, but Rosie stood out.

At the bowling alley, she let a boy help her with her shoes. Then she picked a sparkly pink ball to bowl with.

Rosie was a natural. She bowled strikes while her classmates cheered.

Two popular girls at school, Chelsea and Brooke, were worried. If Rosie got too popular, she might be voted a homecoming princess.

Chelsea wanted to embarrass Rosie. She got Rosie a job at her dad's frozen-yogurt shop.

At the shop, Rosie didn't know how to work the yogurt machine. A lot of people were waiting in line.

Then Chelsea flipped a switch. Yogurt spilled all over the floor . . . and all over Rosie.

Carter was tired of Chelsea and Brooke being so mean. Rosie hadn't done anything to them.

"I am not a fool," said Rosie. "She cannot make something of me that I am not."

She marched up to Chelsea. "Your father would be very disappointed in you," Rosie said. Then she quit her job.

Later, the girls watched the sunset from a pier.

"Thank you for helping me today," said Rosie. "A princess is never sure who is a friend. Today I am sure."

The next day, both girls were picked as homecoming princesses.

"Me being a princess isn't normal," Carter told Rosie.

Then a boy Carter liked asked Rosie to the dance!

Rosie turned him down, but Carter still felt terrible.

Luckily, Rosie wouldn't let one boy get Carter down.

"You are a princess now," Rosie said. "You just do not feel like one yet. . . . It is my turn to teach you."

Carter and Rosie started tutoring their classmates. They read to children at the local library. Then they donated old clothing to a charity thrift shop.

Helping others made Carter feel better about herself.

At the shop, Rosie and Carter each picked a dress to wear to the dance.

In Costa Luna, General Kane announced he was going to marry Rosie's mother. It was a trick to get Rosie to come back.

When Rosie read about the wedding, she wanted to go home. So Carter made a plan to keep Rosie safe. First she convinced Rosie to stay until homecoming.

Then Carter and Rosie helped lots of girls from school by giving them makeovers for the dance.

Carter called Mr. Elegante. He had designed Rosie's dresses in Costa Luna. He sent Carter two dresses. He told General Kane that Rosie would be at the dance, wearing a blue dress.

When General Kane arrived at the dance, he found a room full of princesses. Carter, Rosie, and the girls they had helped were all wearing masks.

General Kane and his men seized the girl in a blue dress. They did not know it was Carter.

Rosie won homecoming queen. Then she realized Carter was missing. She got to Carter just in time.

"This is my fight, not yours," Rosie said.

Major Mason and a group of P.P.P agents captured General Kane. Rosie could finally go home.

Soon Rosie returned to her country, where she was crowned queen of Costa Luna. Carter and her dad went to the ceremony.

"Long live Queen Rosie!" Carter cheered.

Rosie and Carter had helped each other—and they had become friends, too!